Note to parents, carers and teachers

Read it yourself is a series of modern stories, favourite characters and traditional tales written in a simple way for children who are learning to read. The books can be read independently or as part of a guided reading session.

Each book is carefully structured to include many high-frequency words vital for first reading. The sentences on each page are supported closely by pictures to help with understanding, and to offer lively details to talk about.

The books are graded into four levels that progressively introduce wider vocabulary and longer stories as a reader's ability and confidence grows.

Ideas for use

- Begin by looking through the book and talking about the pictures. Has your child heard this story before?

- Help your child with any words he does not know, either by helping him to sound them out or supplying them yourself.

- Developing readers can be concentrating so hard on the words that they sometimes don't fully grasp the meaning of what they're reading. Answering the puzzle questions on pages 30 and 31 will help with understanding.

For more information and advice on Read it yourself and book banding, visit **www.ladybird.com/readityourself**

Book
Band
7

Level 2 is ideal for children who have received some reading instruction and can read short, simple sentences with help.

Special features:

Frequent repetition of main story words and phrases

Short, simple sentences

It was Jack's first day at pirate school.

Time to go!

6

7

Large, clear type

There was the Pirate School ship. All aboard!

"Come on, Jack!" said Miss Crossbones. "All aboard the Pirate School ship."

Careful match between story and pictures

Pirate School

WELCOME PIRATES

8

Educational Consultant: Geraldine Taylor
Book Banding Consultant: Kate Ruttle

A catalogue record for this book is available from the British Library

Published by Ladybird Books Ltd
80 Strand, London, WC2R 0RL
A Penguin Company

001

ISBN: 978-0-71819-467-3

Printed in China

Pirate School

Written by Mandy Ross
Illustrated by Kim Geyer

It was Jack's first day at pirate school.

Time to go!

There was the Pirate School
ship. All aboard!

"Come on, Jack!" said Miss
Crossbones. "All aboard the
Pirate School ship."

"It's time for the first lesson," said Miss Crossbones. "Come and read the treasure map." They all read the treasure map.

"Tip-top! Now it's time for the next lesson," said Miss Crossbones. "How to rescue a pirate."

Jack rescued Ella. Then Ella rescued Jack.

"Tip-top! Now it's time for the next lesson," said Miss Crossbones. "How pirates sail a ship. First, the ship's anchor is pulled up."

They all pulled up the ship's anchor. Then they sailed out to sea, past Shark Waters and Danger Deeps.

"Look!" said Jack. "It's Pirate Island!"

"Put down the ship's anchor," said Miss Crossbones. "Now, all look for the treasure!"

"Where will it be?" said Jack.

They looked here. They looked there. They looked all over the island.

At last, Jack said, "Here's the treasure! It was down a deep hole, just like on the map."

All aboard! They pulled up the ship's anchor and sailed back out to sea.

"Where is Miss Crossbones?" said Ella. "Is she back on Pirate Island?"

They sailed all the way back, past Shark Waters and Danger Deeps.

Danger Deeps

Shark Waters

The pirates looked here.
They looked there. They
looked all over the island.

23

"Help! Help!" said Miss Crossbones.

"Look!" said Jack. "She is down this deep hole! We will rescue you, Miss Crossbones!"

They all rescued Miss
Crossbones, just like
the lesson.

"Tip-top!" said Miss
Crossbones. "Now, all
aboard the ship!"

The pirates sailed all the way back, past Danger Deeps and Shark Waters... just in time!

"A tip-top first day at Pirate School!" said Miss Crossbones.

How much do you remember about the story of Pirate School? Answer these questions and find out!

- **Where does Jack go to school?**

- **What is the name of his teacher?**

- **Which two places do the pirates sail past?**

- **Where do they find the treasure?**

Look at the pictures and match them to the story words.

Jack

Ella

Miss Crossbones

treasure

pirate ship

Read it yourself with Ladybird

Tick the books you've read!

For beginner readers who can read short, simple sentences with help.

Level 2

- Beauty and the Beast ☐
- Chicken Licken ☐
- Little Red Riding Hood ☐
- Nature Trail ☐
- Sports Day ☐
- Pirate School ☐
- Rumpelstiltskin ☐
- Sleeping Beauty ☐
- The Gingerbread Man ☐
- Sly Fox and Red Hen ☐
- The Tale of Jemima Puddle-Duck ☐
- The Three Little Pigs ☐
- Why Lion ROARRRS! ☐
- The Big Race ☐
- Town Mouse and Country Mouse ☐
- Don's Dragon ☐

For more confident readers who can read simple stories with help.

Level 3

- You Won't Like This Present as Much as I Do! ☐
- The Elves and the Shoemaker ☐
- Hansel and Gretel ☐
- Harry and the Bucketful of Dinosaurs ☐
- Jack and the Beanstalk ☐
- Furi on Music Island ☐
- Poppet Stows Away ☐
- Rapunzel ☐
- The Red Knight ☐

Available on the App Store

The Read it yourself with Ladybird app is now available for iPad, iPhone and iPod touch

App also available on Android devices